Where's Gran?

A Tamarind Book

Published by Tamarind Ltd
PO Box 296
Camberley
Surrey GU15 4WD
England

Edited by Huw Wilkins

ISBN   1- 870516 -37 -0

Designed and typeset by Judith Gordon
Originated by Reprospeed, UK
Printed in Singapore

For Gran,
who gave my brother and myself
an enduring love of books and so much else.
And for you, Jellybean, with love.

Where's Gran?

David Rhys

Illustrated by Lynne Willey

Tamarind Ltd

This is Gran's house.
It's far away from town
so Mum is taking her shopping.

Gran's house is full of all sorts – and two fantastic cats.

Gran thinks enormous shops are scary.

'Don't get lost Joe,' said Mum.
'I won't,' said Joe.
'Won't,' said Hannah.
(But that's the only word Hannah can say.)

Gran sometimes talks to herself.

'Who buys all this stuff?' she muttered.

'Where's Gran?' asked Mum.

Joe pointed.
Hannah and
Humphrey bear
also pointed.

LOST PROPERTY ▷

Everyone looked everywhere.

Gran was not in beachwear.

She was not in shoes.
Gran was not in hats.

'Where's Gran?
Is she lost forever?'
wailed Joe.

'Let's go to Lost Property.
Humphrey went there
when Hannah lost him.
Remember?'

'I've lost ...' said Joe.

'We have hats and mats
brollies and trolleys,'
said the woman quickly.

Joe tried again.
'I've lost my ...'

'... books and hooks.
snakes and rakes,'
said the woman.

'*I've lost my Gran,*' said Joe, as fast as he could.
'Oh, dear! Your Gran!' said the lost property woman.

'Have you tried this way?' she asked.

They found
curtains and covers
pots and pans
toys for toddlers.
No Gran.

'Let's get out of here,' said Mum.
'This is a danger zone.'
There were cups and saucers
and breakable things.

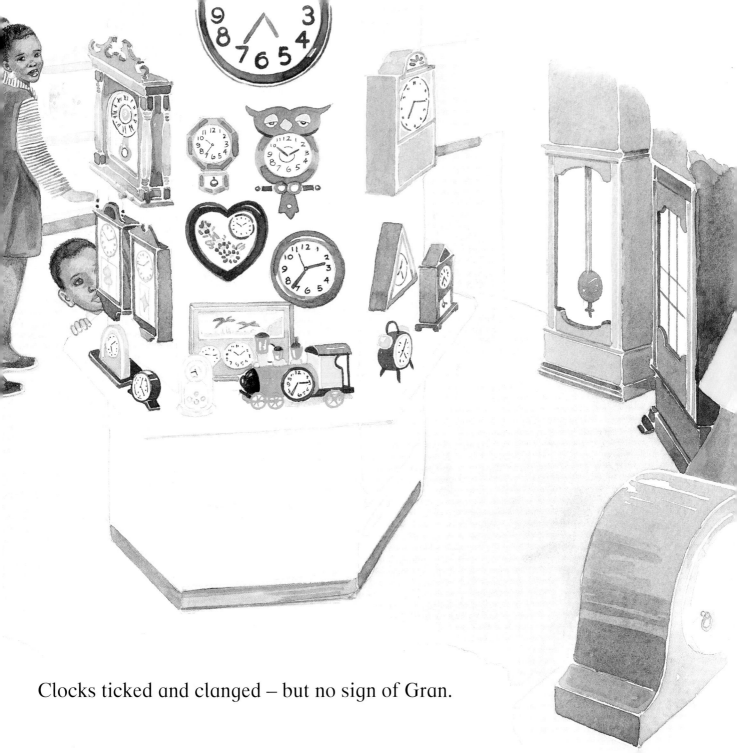

Clocks ticked and clanged – but no sign of Gran.

Then Joe remembered something.
'Books. Gran loves books!'

BOOKS ⟶

'Let's look,'
said Joe and
Mum together.
'Yes, let's look,' said
the woman from
Lost Property.

They searched among the cookery books
and among the gardening books.
They searched in fiction ...

and in fact,   they searched
and searched
and ...

'Here she is!' they all said together.
'Oh Gran, we found you!' said Joe.

'Found me?' said Gran.
'I'm not lost.
I'll buy some of these.
There's great stuff here.'

Soon they were
lost in a story
about cats
and rats
and castles in the air.

coffee shop
←

On the book: **Hide and Seek**

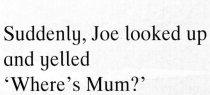

Suddenly, Joe looked up
and yelled
'Where's Mum?'

About the Author

David Rhys is a first time author.
He lives and works in Oxford as a Consultant in the computer world.
This title brings to life his comic genius and love for words.

About the Illustrator

Lynne Willey has produced many bestselling picture books.
Her brilliant illustrations in *I don't Eat Toothpaste Anymore* won the Gold Award
for Best Product at the Nursery & Creche Exhibition.

OTHER TAMARIND TITLES

Jessica

Yohance and the Dinosaurs

Time for Bed

Toyin Fay

Dave and the Tooth Fairy

Kay's Birthday Numbers

Mum Can Fix It

Ben Makes a Cake

Kim's Magic Tree

Time to Get Up

Finished Being Four

ABC – I Can Be

I Don't Eat Toothpaste Anymore

Giant Hiccups

Boots for a Bridesmaid

Are We There Yet?

Kofi and the Butterflies

Abena and the Rock –Ghanian Story

The Snowball Rent – Scottish Story

Five Things to Find – Tunisian Story

Just a Pile of Rice – Chinese Story